To Mark
Love Faye

A Ladybird Book
Series 654

D0955402

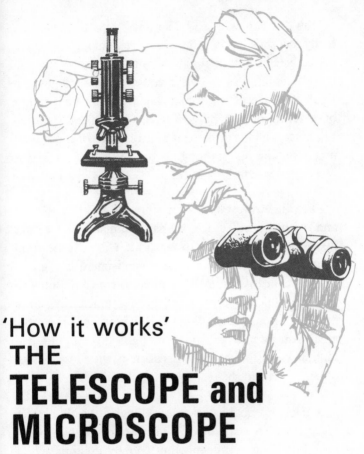

'How it works'
THE
TELESCOPE and
MICROSCOPE

by ROY WORVILL, M.Sc.
with illustrations by B. H. ROBINSON

Publishers: Ladybird Books Ltd . Loughborough
© Ladybird Books Ltd (formerly Wills & Hepworth Ltd) 1971
Printed in England

Two worlds to explore

How far can you see? The answer to this question really depends upon what you are looking at. On a perfectly clear, dark night, if your sight is keen and there is nothing in the way, you can see the light of a small electric bulb, or even a candle-flame, at a distance of several miles. The sun is an object of dazzling brilliance which can be seen at a distance of more than ninety million miles, though—for the sake of one's eyes —it is not wise to look at the sun.

Even the nearest star is far more distant than the sun and, with the naked eye, we can see many whose light takes hundreds of years to reach us. High overhead on winter evenings in the northern hemisphere is a group of stars called Andromeda. Among them is a faint wisp of light which comes from the combined rays of a hundred thousand million stars which make up the great Andromeda galaxy. This light takes about two million years to reach the earth. It is the most distant object which can be seen with the unaided eye.

A telescope enables us to see things at vastly greater distances even than this. A microscope enables us to look into a quite different, but equally exciting, world of things too small for the naked eye. In this book we shall explore both worlds, the very big one shown to us by the telescope and the very small one revealed by the microscope.

0 7214 0294 1

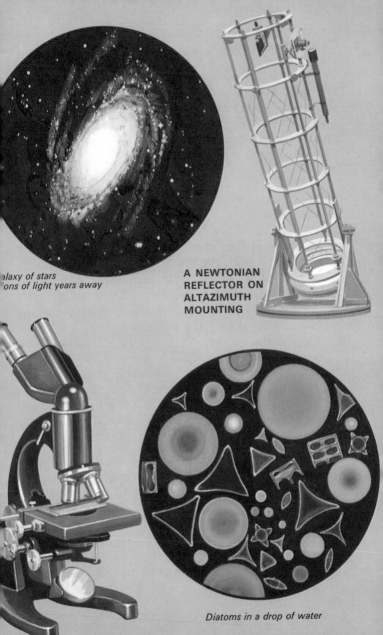

galaxy of stars
...ons of light years away

A NEWTONIAN REFLECTOR ON ALTAZIMUTH MOUNTING

Diatoms in a drop of water

The first telescopes

The earliest telescopes were made about the year 1608. We cannot be sure who made the very first one. Glass lenses were being used for spectacles before this time and two Englishmen, Roger Bacon (1210-1294) and Leonard Digges (1510-1555) who both lived at Oxford, made many experiments with lenses and mirrors.

It seems very probable, however, that the possibility of the telescope was realized by a Dutch spectacle-maker named Hans Lippershey, although a fellow-countryman of the same trade, Zacharias Jansen, also claimed the credit. The discovery was almost certainly the result of a simple experiment using two lenses. Distant objects suddenly appeared to be nearer. This would obviously be very useful in time of war, enabling an enemy to be watched at a distance.

Perhaps you have used a simple convex lens as a burning-glass, collecting the sun's rays and concentrating their light and heat in a small bright spot. This spot is a very small picture, or image, of the sun. The distance from the spot to the lens is called the focal length of the lens.

An image formed in this way can be magnified by another lens, of shorter focal length, and this is most conveniently done by mounting both lenses in a tube.

Some of the first telescopes were very long, as much as 150 feet, in order to avoid the worst effects of rainbow-coloured edges, produced because a simple lens cannot bring all the colours in sunlight to the same focal point.

Galileo explores the heavens

News about the wonderful new invention quickly spread to countries outside Holland; to France, Germany and Italy. In Venice it reached the ears of an Italian professor of mathematics named Galileo Galilei. He is usually known by his first name, Galileo, and it was he who first gave the new instrument the name 'telescope', meaning an instrument to see things at a distance.

Galileo set to work to make a telescope for his own use. It magnified only about three times, but it astonished the noblemen of Venice as they surveyed their city's buildings and ships from church-tower balconies.

After more experiments, Galileo succeeded in making a much better telescope which magnified about thirty times, and early in the year 1610 he began to look at the sky. He made some surprising and important discoveries.

The landscape of the moon was seen to have mountain ranges and craters great and small. The planet Jupiter was found to have four smaller worlds, its satellites, revolving round it. The bright planet Venus showed a crescent phase like the moon, and Saturn had something close to it which the telescope could not clearly show. Only later, with the aid of better telescopes, was it possible to see Saturn's spectacular system of rings. The pale band of light crossing the sky, which we call the Milky Way, was seen to come from vast numbers of stars.

The telescope had become an instrument for the discoveries of science and not just a weapon of war.

GALILEO'S TELESCOPE had a concave eye-lens and gave an upright image.

*...lileo's drawing of the moon
...he saw it through his telescope.*

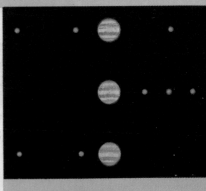

*Jupiter and its satellites as
Galileo saw them on different nights.*

The lens makes the picture

Our own eyes are rather like a telescope, and also like a camera, in the way they work. They have a lens at the front which collects light coming from the object we are looking at and brings it to a focus on the retina at the back of the eye. This acts as a kind of screen, where the image, or picture, is formed. Like the image formed by the lens of a telescope or a camera, it is upside-down. We see the object the right way up because, in a wonderful way, our brain turns it round.

The large, front lens of a telescope is called the object-glass, or the objective. It is very much larger than the pupil of our eye and so it collects much more light. A lens of two inches diameter, for example, collects about one hundred times more light than our eye normally receives. The light is bent, or refracted, as it passes through the lens and brought to a focus at a distance which is the focal length of the lens. Here, as we have seen, the image is made. If we hold a sheet of paper at this point we can see the image of an object, such as a distant light bulb, projected on the screen of paper.

The telescope also has a smaller lens of much shorter focal length and placed just behind the focus of the objective lens. This is the eyepiece and it gives a magnified view of the object. It is sometimes thought that high magnification is the most important thing about a telescope, but this is not entirely true. Astronomers, especially, may need very large lenses in order to see objects which are too faint or too distant to be seen with small ones, but they do not always use high powers of magnification.

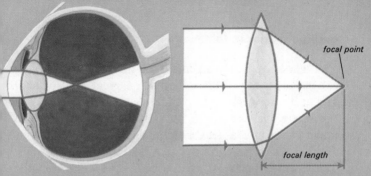

Our eyes have a convex lens to focus the light.

A convex lens makes light rays converge.

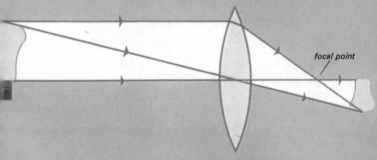

HOW THE OBJECT LENS FORMS AN INVERTED IMAGE
In practice the focal length would be much greater than shown. For simplicity, two rays of light are shown from the upper part of the bulb, but in fact all parts of the lens receive light to form the image.

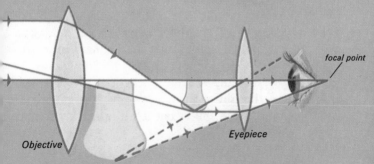

HOW THE EYEPIECE MAGNIFIES THE IMAGE

Making a simple telescope

A good optical instrument of any kind is usually expensive to buy. This is because a great deal of skill and accurate work go into the making and mounting of the lenses, prisms and other parts. However, you can make a telescope at least as good as the best one used by Galileo when he carried out his famous observations. The essential parts, which can be bought quite cheaply, are two convex lenses and two strong, cardboard postal tubes. One tube must be slightly larger than the object-glass and the other should be of smaller size to slide easily, but not loosely, inside it.

A lens of one inch diameter and about twelve inches in focal length will do, but a much better size would be two inches in diameter. It should have a focal length of about twenty or thirty inches. It is mounted an inch or two from one end of the larger tube and may be held in place between two short sections of smaller tube. The larger tube should have a length of about 32 inches, or an inch or two longer than the focal length of the object-glass.

The small lens, which forms the magnifier or eyepiece, is placed close to one end of the shorter, smaller tube which should be about four or five inches long. If the eye-lens has a focal length of one inch our telescope will give a magnification of thirty times, or thirty diameters as it is sometimes called. This figure is obtained by dividing the focal length of the eyepiece into that of the object-glass. A two-inch eyepiece will only magnify fifteen times, but it will normally have a wider field of view.

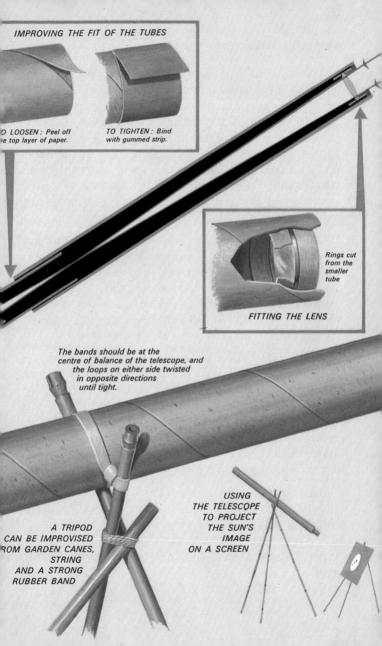

IMPROVING THE FIT OF THE TUBES

TO LOOSEN : Peel off the top layer of paper.

TO TIGHTEN : Bind with gummed strip.

Rings cut from the smaller tube

FITTING THE LENS

The bands should be at the centre of balance of the telescope, and the loops on either side twisted in opposite directions until tight.

A TRIPOD CAN BE IMPROVISED FROM GARDEN CANES, STRING AND A STRONG RUBBER BAND

USING THE TELESCOPE TO PROJECT THE SUN'S IMAGE ON A SCREEN

Using the telescope

After testing the performance of your two-inch telescope it is a good idea to see how it works when you 'stop' down the lens. This means covering up the outer part by means of a circular piece of black paper or cardboard, leaving a central hole with a diameter of $1\frac{1}{2}$ inches. This will almost certainly improve the definition or sharpness of the image. It will also reduce the false colour. Some of the light will be lost, of course, since part of the lens is covered, but the magnification will still be the same.

What will the telescope show you? If you look at a tree or building you will notice at once that it appears upside-down. To show it the right way up a special kind of lens or prism called an erecting, or terrestrial, eyepiece is needed. But this is not necessary if we are looking at the sky, and in any case extra lenses absorb some of the light.

Never look directly at the sun with any optical instrument. If you want to see the sunspots, use the telescope as a projector with a sheet of white card or paper for a screen. The moon will show its mountain ranges and craters clearly, except when it is full. At full moon there are no dark shadows to provide contrast. Jupiter will be seen as a small, yellow disc with the four largest satellites which Galileo discovered.

Saturn's rings may just be glimpsed if the telescope is supported steadily, and the brilliant planet Venus will show its crescent like a very small moon. As for the stars, the telescope will show at least 300,000 on a clear night, compared with the 2,000 visible to the unaided eye.

14

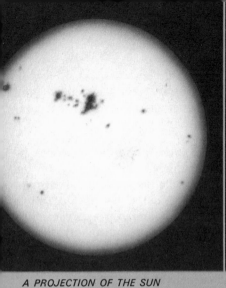

A PROJECTION OF THE SUN

THE MOON

JUPITER WITH THREE OF ITS SATELLITES

VENUS

SATURN

Isaac Newton's mirror telescope

Even very clever men make mistakes. Isaac Newton (1642-1727) was one of our greatest scientists and mathematicians, but one of his most important contributions to science arose from an error.

All attempts to make more powerful telescopes by using larger lenses encountered the difficulty of the coloured rainbow which the lens produced around bright objects like the moon and the planets. Our simple telescope cannot avoid these coloured fringes caused by the lens refracting different colours unequally, just as drops of water produce a rainbow in the sky. The lens brings the violet and blue rays of light to a focus nearer to the lens itself than it does the red light.

Newton thought that this difficulty could never be overcome by any kind of lens. He was not quite correct in thinking this, but it led him to the use of a mirror to form an image, and so to build the reflecting telescope which still bears his name, the Newtonian reflector.

A curved mirror will bring rays of light to a focus and form an image by reflection just as the lens does by bending or refraction. There is an important difference, however, because the mirror brings all the rays together, whatever their colour, if the curve of its surface is made in the shape called a paraboloid. The reflector in a motor-car headlight is curved in this way although its purpose is different from that of the telescope mirror.

Many of the world's great telescopes have been made on the pattern of Isaac Newton's and their use has led to many discoveries in astronomy.

Sir Isaac Newton
(1642-1727)

NEWTON'S REFLECTING TELESCOPE

A NEWTONIAN REFLECTOR ON A
FORK-TYPE EQUATORIAL MOUNT

Eyepiece

Elliptical flat mirror

Concave mirror

The rival telescopes

There are many different kinds of lenses. They differ not only in size and the way they are shaped but also in the kinds of glass used to make them. Isaac Newton made the mistake of thinking that all lenses would be troubled by rainbows of false colour, but it was later discovered that the faults of one lens can be made to correct, at least partially, the faults of another. In optical instruments, two mistakes of opposite kinds can sometimes give us a right answer, just as they can in arithmetic.

About 1730 an Englishman named Chester Moor Hall discovered that a lens made in two parts and of two different kinds of glass, one called crown glass and the other flint glass, avoided much of the unwanted colour. Very little notice seems to have been taken of this discovery and it was only after another 25 years that an optician, John Dollond, announced that he had made an achromatic, or colour-free, object-glass. However, it was left to a young German, Joseph Fraunhofer, to develop the discovery, and his $9\frac{1}{2}$ inch Dorpat refractor, produced in 1825, surpassed all other instruments.

Much later still it was discovered that the addition of a third lens, using three different kinds of glass, gave a still greater improvement and, because these lenses can be used equally well for photography or for observation, they are called photovisual lenses.

In addition to these improvements, almost all lenses made now are given a coating which can be seen as a blue, purple or amber-coloured reflection. This coating, or 'blooming', allows much more light to pass through the lens by reducing the loss of rays reflected at the surfaces.

With the discovery of the achromatic lens the battle between the object-glass and the mirror began, and each still has its champions today.

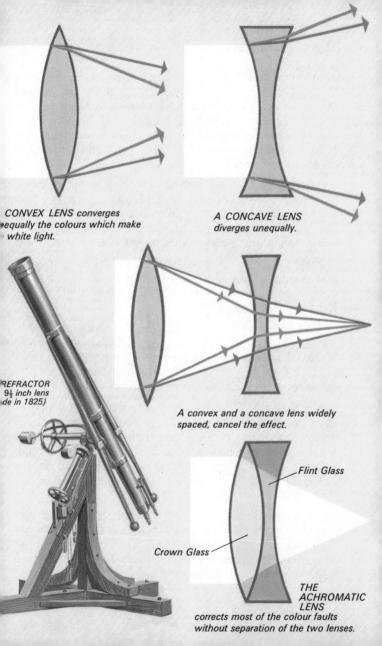

CONVEX LENS converges equally the colours which make white light.

A CONCAVE LENS diverges unequally.

REFRACTOR
9½ inch lens
made in 1825)

A convex and a concave lens widely spaced, cancel the effect.

Flint Glass

Crown Glass

THE ACHROMATIC LENS
corrects most of the colour faults without separation of the two lenses.

The big reflectors

In the year 1757, only months before John Dollond announced his new object-glass, a musician named William Herschel came from Hanover, in Germany, to live in London. Later he moved to Bath where he quickly became famous for his musical activities. He began to take an interest in astronomy and decided to make a telescope.

After more than a hundred experiments which ended in failure, he succeeded in making a mirror which worked well. The mirror, like all telescope mirrors at this time, was made not of glass but of metal. It was called speculum metal, a mixture of copper and tin.

Following this success he became more ambitious and made a number of larger mirrors. At last he completed a mirror which was the biggest ever made. It had a diameter of 48 inches.

An enormous telescope was built at Slough in Buckinghamshire, but, like many men before and since, Herschel found that big things often bring their own problems and for much of his work he found a smaller telescope with a 6½ inch mirror more useful.

His greatest discovery was made with a telescope of this size when, in March, 1781, he found the new planet which is called Uranus. With the devoted help of his sister Caroline, who recorded his observations through freezing nights when even the ink froze hard in the bottle, he also made many important discoveries among the stars.

Since Herschel's time, telescopes have grown bigger still. There are two with mirrors of 200 inches diameter and more. The 200-inch telescope is on Palomar Mountain in California. In Russia there is an even larger one which uses a mirror of 236 inches diameter.

Tilted mirror

**HERSCHEL'S
48 inch
REFLECTING
TELESCOPE**

Sir William Herschel
(1738-1822)

Other kinds of telescope

Not all reflecting telescopes are made like that first invented by Isaac Newton. There are several other designs, some of which are used for special purposes such as photographing the sun and stars. Large telescopes are often made in a way first suggested by a Frenchman named Cassegrain in 1672. Two curved mirrors are used as shown in the diagram, and the observer stands at the lower end of the tube as with the refracting telescope.

Another telescope, which looks very much like the Cassegrain design, was suggested by a Scottish mathematician named James Gregory, in 1663. No-one succeeded in making a telescope exactly to Gregory's design until some years later, and they are seldom seen today except in museums. The Gregorian telescope, with its short tube and tripod of polished brass, is now little more than an ornament.

The Mount Palomar telescope is made in the form of the Cassegrain with a skeleton tube large enough for the astronomer to sit inside it, near the focus of the mirror, to photograph the stars. Britain's largest telescope is at the Royal Observatory, Herstmonceux, Sussex. This has a mirror of 96 inches diameter and is called the Isaac Newton Memorial telescope. It is perhaps strange that although built to commemorate the genius of Isaac Newton, it is also made in the form designed by the Frenchman, Cassegrain.

Several forms of the Cassegrain telescope are in use. One of these, known as the Maksutov, after its Russian designer, is shown in the illustration. It has the advantage of being very compact and, because it uses a lens as well as a mirror to form the image, is sometimes called a catadioptric telescope.

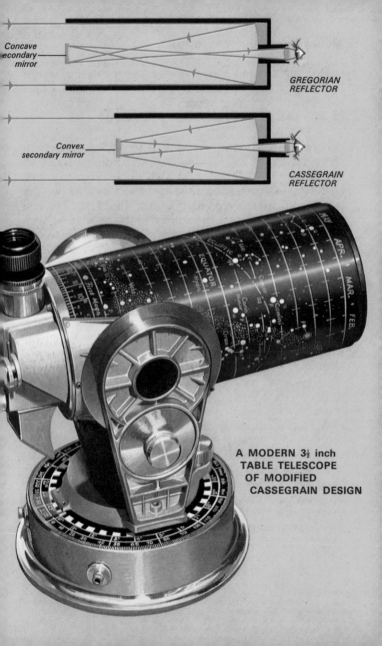

Concave secondary mirror

GREGORIAN REFLECTOR

Convex secondary mirror

CASSEGRAIN REFLECTOR

A MODERN 3½ inch
TABLE TELESCOPE
OF MODIFIED
CASSEGRAIN DESIGN

Mountings and accessories

Holding any but a very small telescope in the hand is both tiring and difficult. We need a firm and steady support as well as a means of pointing the telescope easily towards the object being observed.

A telescope used for looking at the moon, planets or stars must be kept moving almost continuously. It is not the motion of the moon itself through space which is the main reason for this, but the fact that we are watching it from a moving platform, the earth. The east to west movement of the sun or moon may seem slow to the unaided sight but when we use a telescope we are magnifying this motion, and the area of sky which we see through the eyepiece is always very small. The more we magnify, the smaller this area becomes, and the faster the object appears to move. Of course, if we are looking at something on the earth, a distant church clock for example, this movement does not take place. The observer and the clock are moving together at the same speed. There is no relative movement between them.

A telescope mount which enables us to make simple movements in horizontal and vertical directions is called an altazimuth mount. Large astronomical telescopes, and occasionally small ones, are used on an equatorial mount. This has one axis arranged so that it is parallel to the axis of the earth. The telescope then follows the object in a smooth, curved path and needs only one movement instead of two. This movement is often done mechanically by a weight-driven clock or an electric motor. A small telescope, called a finder, is usually attached to the large tube, enabling an object to be found quickly in the main telescope. It has cross wires to mark the centre.

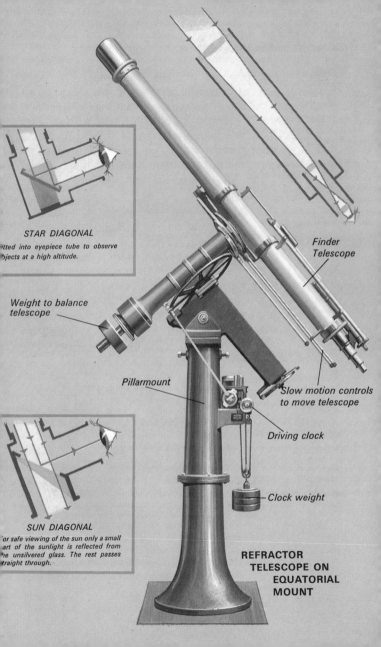

STAR DIAGONAL

Fitted into eyepiece tube to observe objects at a high altitude.

Finder Telescope

Weight to balance telescope

Pillarmount

Slow motion controls to move telescope

Driving clock

Clock weight

SUN DIAGONAL

For safe viewing of the sun only a small part of the sunlight is reflected from the unsilvered glass. The rest passes straight through.

REFRACTOR TELESCOPE ON EQUATORIAL MOUNT

Observatories and their work

Large telescopes and observatories, placed on high mountain tops, are not intended for astronomers to sit up all night looking at the moon and planets. This kind of observation can be done almost as well with smaller telescopes. However, when the air is very still, which does not often happen, a large telescope will show smaller objects on the moon or a planet than one of lesser size. The larger one is said to have greater resolving power.

The big lens or mirror of a large telescope is made for the purpose of collecting more light, just as the roof of a building collects more rainwater than a bucket. The 200-inch mirror of the Mount Palomar telescope collects a million times more light than our eyes, because its surface is so much larger. This means that it enables a watcher to see very faint stars which are far beyond the reach of the naked eye. It reveals the stars and galaxies in distant regions of space from which light takes many millions of years to reach us.

An astronomer may seldom look through his telescope. Instead of his eye, he uses a photographic plate to make pictures of the sky. Before the days of photography astronomers had to draw pictures of what they saw. A drawing, however, depends upon the care and accuracy of the artist, and his eye may deceive him very easily if the object is very small or faint. The photographic plate or film has a great advantage. It can face a distant star for hours on end and it will go on storing up the light to make a brighter picture.

Opposite (1) The largest refractor in the world —
a 40-inch telescope at Yerkes Observatory, Wisconsin, U.S.A.

(2) The 200-inch reflector telescope at Mount Palomar.

Prime focus
for photographs
and observing
faint stars

observation of
ight stars

mirror

ronomer taking photographs at prime focus.

1

The radio telescope

Optical telescopes, by which we mean those using light to form a magnified image of distant objects, have now been with us for nearly four hundred years. The radio telescope is a much more recent invention and has been in use for less than forty years. Perhaps the name 'telescope' is not a very good one for it, since we see nothing except a wavy line made by a pen travelling across a moving strip of paper. Nevertheless, the radio telescope has enabled astronomers to find out much new information about far-off stars and galaxies.

We can think of an optical telescope as a window from which we look out into space. The radio telescope enables us to open the window more widely. It collects radio waves which reach us from space and to which our eyes are quite blind.

Britain's best-known radio telescope is the great bowl at Jodrell Bank in Cheshire, but not all radio telescopes are built like this. Some have aerials built in long lines like telephone wires. The radio telescope cannot show us what any object looks like but it can reach out much further into space than even the largest lens or mirror.

It is important to remember that when we look at the sky we are looking back in time, as well as into the far distance. We see even the nearest star as it was over four years ago. With the radio telescope turned towards the sky, astronomers are able to receive radio waves which left the stars many millions of years before the light rays of the most distant visible stars.

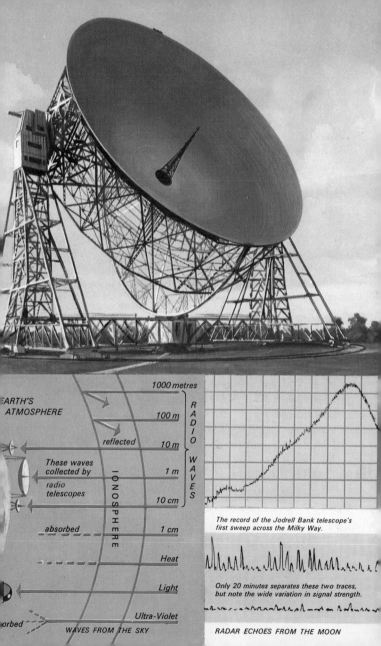

EARTH'S
ATMOSPHERE

1000 metres
100 m
10 m

R A D I O

reflected

These waves
collected by

1 m

radio
telescopes

10 cm

W A V E S

I O N O S P H E R E

absorbed

1 cm

Heat

Light

Ultra-Violet

orbed

WAVES FROM THE SKY

*The record of the Jodrell Bank telescope's
first sweep across the Milky Way.*

*Only 20 minutes separates these two traces,
but note the wide variation in signal strength.*

RADAR ECHOES FROM THE MOON

Binoculars

If we place two similar telescopes side by side, so that their tubes are exactly parallel, we can use both eyes instead of one. This arrangement forms a pair of binoculars and it has some advantages over the ordinary monocular telescope. We are normally used to seeing with both eyes. Though close together they are looking at things from slightly different positions, and this gives us the very valuable advantage of what is called stereoscopic vision. Things stand out instead of looking like part of a flat picture.

Some binoculars are still made like two of Galileo's telescopes put together, but quite short. Small opera glasses are often made like this. For most purposes, however, a much better, though more expensive form, is the prismatic binocular. In this form of twin telescope there are prisms which have the effect of folding the light-rays and keeping the instrument small enough to be easily held in the hand.

Like the ordinary telescope, binoculars have object-glasses at the front to form the image and eyepieces to magnify, and the larger the object-glass the brighter will be the image. On one of the two small plates which cover the prisms, near the eyepiece, there are normally two figures given. They may be shown as 6×30, 7×50, 8×40 or 10×50. In each case, the first figure gives the magnification and the second one is the diameter of the object-glass measured in millimetres.

Although rather low in magnification, binoculars are delightful instruments to use for astronomy, bird-watching, sport or simply looking round the landscape. However, it is essential that the prisms are accurately adjusted to bring both images together.

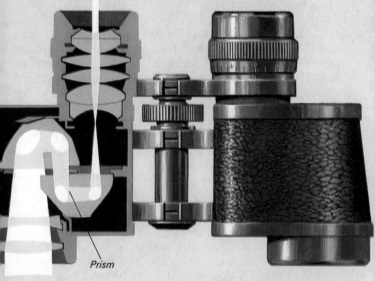

Eyepiece

This eyepiece can be focussed independently to compensate for slight differences in focus of the observer's eyes.

Prism

Objective

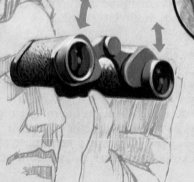

Adjustment to suit individual eye spacing is made by rotating binoculars about their centre.

A wrong view of the binocular field, often shown by films and television.

Correctly adjusted binocular shows one circular field of view.

The first microscopes

Although the purpose of the microscope is quite different from that of the telescope, the two instruments resemble one another in some ways. Both have an object-glass to form an image which is then magnified by another lens, the eyepiece. In fact the eyepiece of the microscope can act very successfully when it is used in a telescope. With my own astronomical telescope, which is a Newtonian reflector having a mirror of $8\frac{1}{2}$ inches diameter, I often use an eyepiece which came from a microscope.

However, the microscope, as its name suggests, is an instrument for magnifying and observing very small objects. Its simplest form is that of an ordinary convex lens which has many advantages if the object being looked at is not too small. The lens need not even be made of glass. A drop of water can be used as a magnifier and you have probably noticed how a very small goldfish looks much bigger when you look at it through the bowl of water which refracts the light passing through it just as a lens does. Lenses for this purpose have also been made by using other transparent liquids, such as clear varnish, while diamonds, sapphires and other precious stones have been similarly used.

As with the telescope, it is uncertain who invented the microscope. Some drawings of natural objects which must have been made with the help of a magnifier were published in Germany before the year 1600, and a Jesuit priest named Kircher, who lived in the middle of the seventeenth century, listed six different kinds of microscope. They included glass bowls and hemispheres filled with water and another made up of two convex glass lenses.

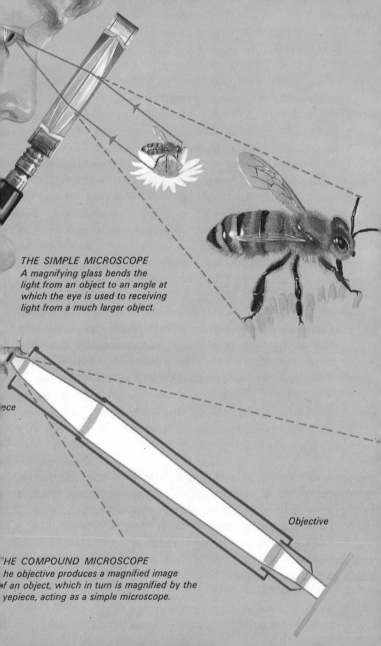

THE SIMPLE MICROSCOPE
A magnifying glass bends the light from an object to an angle at which the eye is used to receiving light from a much larger object.

...iece

Objective

THE COMPOUND MICROSCOPE
*T*he objective produces a magnified image *o*f an object, which in turn is magnified by the *e*yepiece, acting as a simple microscope.

The compound microscope

The name microscope seems to have been first given to a magnifying instrument in the year 1625, although it was not much used for scientific purposes until about 1650. Simple magnifiers were often preferred because they gave a clearer, though smaller image.

The first really good microscope, like the first tele- scope, came from Holland and was made by Antony van Leeuwenhoek (1632-1723). His observations des- cribe objects which were only one ten-thousandth part of an inch, or one four-hundredth part of a millimetre, across. One of his few simple microscopes to survive can be seen in the museum at the University of Leyden, in Holland.

An Englishman named Robert Hooke was one of the first to use the compound microscope for scientific purposes and, in 1665, he published a famous book about his work. In it he has much to say about the beauty of the flea, its body 'adorned all over with a suit of polished armour, neatly-jointed and covered with sharp pins, shaped almost like porcupine's quills or bright steel bodkins'.

Unlike the object-glass of the telescope, the micro- scope's objective is very small. An object being examined must be brightly lit and Hooke used a small oil lamp to illuminate his specimens or, if they were thin enough for light to pass through them (as many microscope specimens are) he had a hole underneath the object to pass the light of a candle.

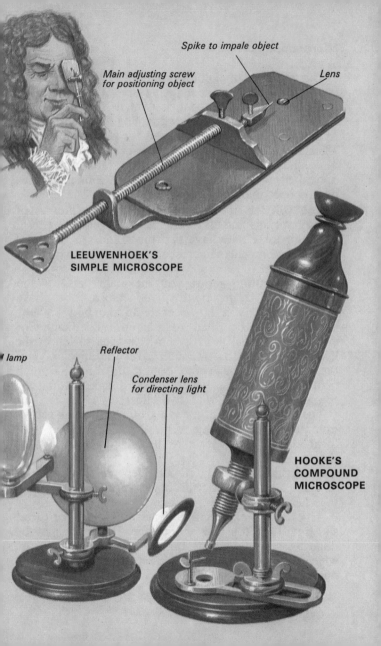

Spike to impale object

Lens

Main adjusting screw
for positioning object

**LEEUWENHOEK'S
SIMPLE MICROSCOPE**

Reflector

lamp

Condenser lens
for directing light

**HOOKE'S
COMPOUND
MICROSCOPE**

Microscopes of today

The rainbow of colour produced by a simple lens troubled the microscope makers just as it did those who made telescopes. Some opticians made both telescopes and microscopes, just as they do today. The achromatic, or colour-free lens was not used for microscopes until 1830. It was another fifty years before the discovery of new kinds of glass first enabled the famous German optical firm of Carl Zeiss to produce a fine, modern microscope objective.

You will see microscopes in the shop windows of many opticians and all follow the same general pattern, although some may have two tubes and sets of lenses if they are binocular microscopes to be used with both eyes.

The illustration shows you the main parts of the instrument with its rigid stirrup-shaped foot above which is usually a hinge enabling the body of the microscope to be tilted to a comfortable angle for viewing. The small mirror can be moved to reflect the light from a window—though *never* the direct rays of the sun—up through the central hole in the small platform or stage on which the glass slide holding the specimen is secured with two clips.

The microscope shown has a group of three objectives mounted in a revolving turret. These are of different focal lengths because, unlike the telescope, in which all the magnifying power is given by the eyepiece, the magnification of the microscope depends upon both of its main optical parts, the objective and the eyepiece together.

An eyepiece, of which there are usually two or three, slides into the top end of the tube. Focussing may be done by a simple sliding tube or, more frequently, by what is called a rack and pinion movement which is operated by the wheel at the side.

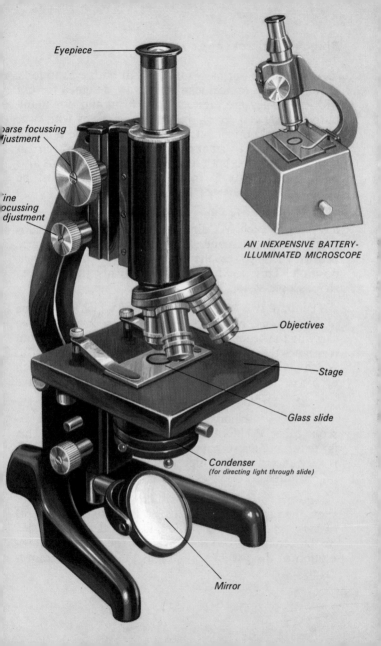

Eyepiece

Coarse focussing adjustment

Fine focussing adjustment

AN INEXPENSIVE BATTERY-ILLUMINATED MICROSCOPE

Objectives

Stage

Glass slide

Condenser
(for directing light through slide)

Mirror

Binocular microscopes

Although we normally make use of both eyes to look at things, most optical instruments are designed for use with one. They are monocular in form and, for many purposes, we can see as well with one eye as with two. A binocular form of telescope or microscope is much more difficult to make successfully and keep in adjustment so that both images merge into one. It is also much more costly to make, since each lens must be duplicated and each pair must match perfectly.

Nevertheless, the binocular instrument has one great advantage which has already been mentioned in connection with telescopes. It gives depth to the image because each eye sees the object from a slightly different position. This is what we have already described as stereoscopic vision.

There are two kinds of microscope which enable the observer to use both eyes. There may be one main tube carrying the beam of light from the objective but, before it reaches the eyepiece, the light passes through a prism which divides it into two parts, one of which goes to each eyepiece. The divided beam, however, does not give true stereoscopic effect.

The other method is to mount two separate microscope tubes, each with its matching sets of lenses. This is the form of microscope shown in the lower picture and is very effective where high powers of magnification are not required.

Another form of binocular microscope is often used to show the rapid movement (called Brownian movement) of very small particles in liquids. The depth produced by binocular vision easily shows the up and down motion of the particles as well as their sideways movement.

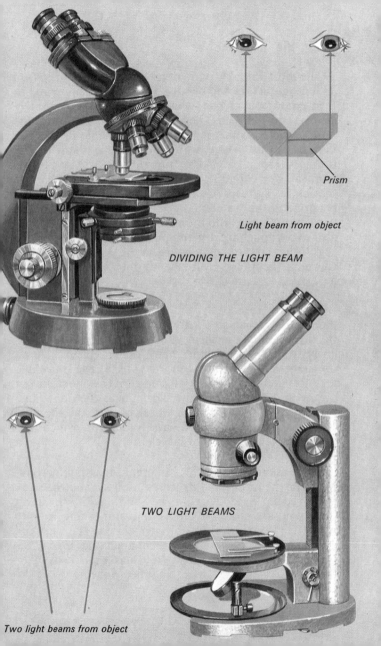

Prism

Light beam from object

DIVIDING THE LIGHT BEAM

TWO LIGHT BEAMS

Two light beams from object

Using the microscope

The most valuable parts of any optical instrument are its lenses, mirrors and prisms. They are usually made of high-grade optical glass which has been very accurately shaped and polished. Glass is a hard material but some dust particles, which may be quite invisible to the eye, may be harder. There are many of these about in any ordinary room and if they are rubbed across the lens surface by careless cleaning, they are liable to scratch the surface. A scratch will stop some of the light passing through and many will ruin the lens. Avoid the temptation to rub a lens every time you use it and also avoid touching it with your fingers. Because of the slightly acid nature of moisture on the skin, finger-marks can etch themselves permanently into the surface of a lens.

If the microscope is not fitted with electric battery illumination, first adjust the mirror by tilting it to get the brightest light in the field of the eyepiece, but always away from direct sunlight. Place the specimen slide on the stage and secure it with the clips. If the objectives are mounted in a revolving turret, turn the one of lowest power to a point above the slide. Focus the image first with the coarse adjustment wheel, then make the final movement with the fine focussing control, which acts like a low gear on a car or bicycle.

Some microscopes have a different focussing mechanism. The main tube and its lenses are fixed and the stage is moved up or down with the slide on it. Whichever type you are using, there is one important rule to remember. Start with the objective close to the slide and get the best focus by moving them apart, never towards one another. Many a good slide has been broken or the objective cracked by forcing them together.

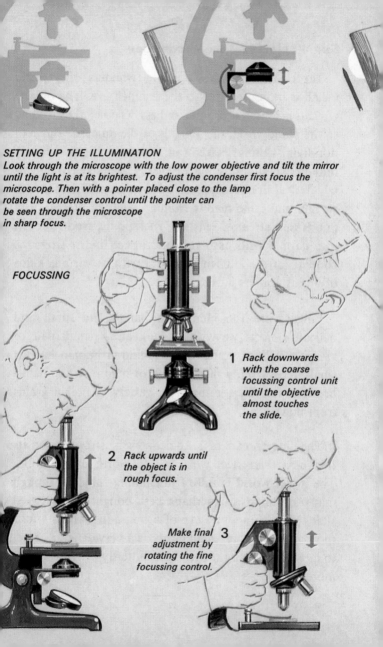

SETTING UP THE ILLUMINATION

Look through the microscope with the low power objective and tilt the mirror until the light is at its brightest. To adjust the condenser first focus the microscope. Then with a pointer placed close to the lamp rotate the condenser control until the pointer can be seen through the microscope in sharp focus.

FOCUSSING

1 *Rack downwards with the coarse focussing control unit until the objective almost touches the slide.*

2 *Rack upwards until the object is in rough focus.*

Make final **3** *adjustment by rotating the fine focussing control.*

Some objects for the microscope

The microscope shows us the wonders of a world which is quite invisible to the unaided eye. The objects we can examine are quite endless whether they belong to the plant world, the animals or the immense range of non-living things. We can choose objects already mounted as slides from a vast array available from firms which deal in microscopes and their accessories. Others we can find quite readily from a variety of places, from ponds and streams, seashore rock-pools, from the soil in a garden with its plants and insect life or from the contents of the kitchen cupboard with its various kinds of grains and crystals.

Fingers are too clumsy to handle the small and delicate objects we wish to look at. A small pair of tweezers will be needed for handling a human hair or small fibres from a piece of silk or nylon. A fine paint-brush is suitable for the great variety of pollen grains from flowers.

The fine thread of a spider's web, stronger for its thickness than steel wire, is well worth examination. The insect world is full of fascinating subjects, though many of these are perhaps best bought as prepared slides. The compound eye of a house-fly, with its four thousand, separate, small facets, is a very delicate object to mount and so is the eye of the butterfly with thousands more facets.

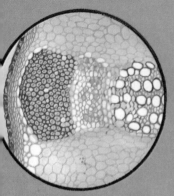

SECTION OF PLANT STEM

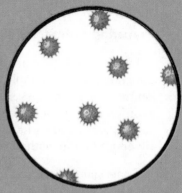

POLLEN GRAINS

PLANT LIFE IN POND WATER

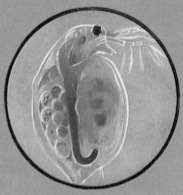

WATER FLEA

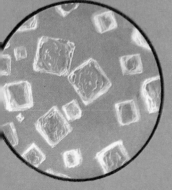

SALT CRYSTALS

FORAMINIFERA

Preparing slides: dry mounting

It is possible to look at some objects, crystals of common salt for example, by placing a thin layer on the centre of a plain glass slide which is then clipped into position on the microscope stage. However, if you wish to prepare a slide which can be kept permanently for observation, the method requires a little more care.

Some small specimens can be mounted in a dry state. This is done by brushing a thin film of clear gum on the centre of the slide, which is a small rectangle of glass, and then leaving it to dry. Then breathe on the gum to soften it slightly and place the specimen centrally in the gummed circle with a fine, moistened paint-brush. The specimen must then be protected by one of the very small and fragile cover slips. To do this a drop of Canada Balsam, specially made for this purpose, is placed on the specimen so that it will stick to the cover slip. In the case of a rather thick object, aluminium rings or cells should be used to raise the cover slip clear of the specimen. The cover slip is then put in place and sealed with shellac ringing cement.

If you look at some of the dry-mounted slides sold by many optical and scientific shops, you will see what the finished slide should look like. Your slide can be labelled for future reference.

Dry mounting means exactly what it says. The specimens must be really dry. If there is any moisture in or on them, it will appear later in small beads on the underside of the cover slip and the slide will then be spoiled.

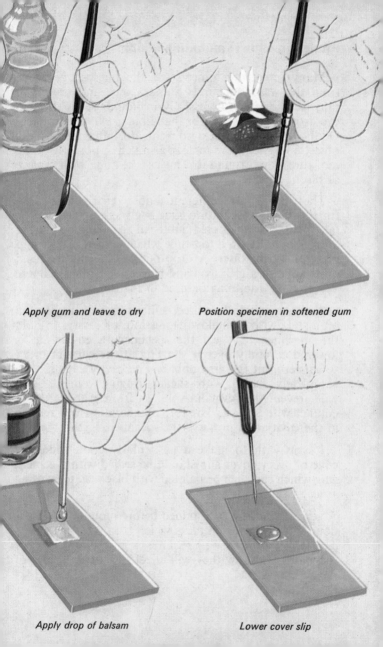

Apply gum and leave to dry

Position specimen in softened gum

Apply drop of balsam

Lower cover slip

Preparing slides: mounting in fluid

Many interesting objects for the microscope come from the water in ponds and streams, and these can only be mounted successfully in liquid. A small glass eye-dropper is useful for handling such a specimen. Oddly enough, the next thing to do, after placing the object on a slide, is to remove as much as possible of the moisture from around it. This can be done with a piece of blotting paper.

There are several different fluids which can be used for this kind of mounting. One is glycerine jelly. This is fairly solid when it is cold but it can be melted by putting a small quantity in a test-tube which is then placed in a glass of warm water. A drop of the liquid is collected on the end of a glass rod and placed over the specimen. Water-glass, too, may be used in the same way.

Another liquid often used is formalin and this is used on a slide with a shallow depression, or cavity, to hold the specimen. To seal the specimen, a cover slip is lowered carefully over it, starting at the edge in order to squeeze out the air bubbles. The cavity edge is then completely sealed with shellac ringing cement. This will prevent the formalin solution from evaporating in contact with the air. The formalin solution will remain in the cavity and preserve the specimen.

If you wish to make a particularly good slide, the edge of every cover slip should be sealed with a cement ring which can then be painted with black lacquer, using a very fine brush.

Some specimens are stained before mounting. This is done to colour certain parts which then stand out more clearly. To do this well requires a good knowledge of the stains and how they will affect the various parts of the specimen.

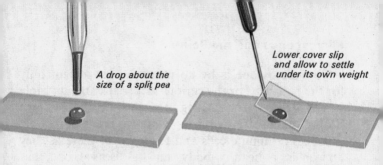

PREPARING A SLIDE FOR THE EXAMINATION OF A FLUID
(e.g. pond water or blood)

A drop about the size of a split pea

Lower cover slip and allow to settle under its own weight

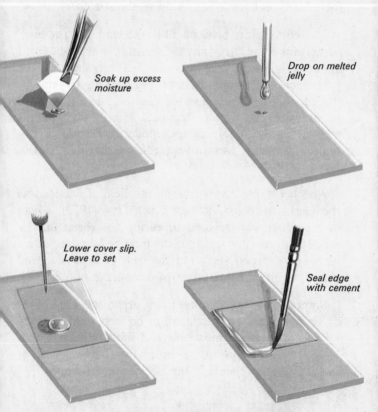

Soak up excess moisture

Drop on melted jelly

Lower cover slip. Leave to set

Seal edge with cement

MOUNTING IN GLYCERINE JELLY

Microscopes and medicine

The microscope is by no means an instrument only for the naturalist or the curious seeker after the invisible world. It has been of the greatest help in the study of health and disease. All living matter is made up of vast numbers of minute cells and the study of these as they appear in a healthy body, and a diseased one, has enabled doctors and scientists to discover much about the causes of illness and, in many cases though unfortunately not yet in all, to bring about a cure.

The connection between ill-health and the presence of certain very tiny micro-organisms was discovered about a hundred years ago in the workshop of the French chemist, Louis Pasteur (1822-1895). His microscopes, like the telescopes of Galileo and other early scientists, would now be regarded as very poor instruments, yet the whole of our modern research in immunisation and preventive medicine, as it is called, began with Pasteur's work.

Another important worker in this field of science was the German doctor, Robert Koch (1843-1910). Much of his effort was devoted to curing the sheep disease called anthrax. For much of the time he laboured at his work in a garden shed and the lack of expensive and elaborate instruments failed to discourage him.

Some of the very smallest living organisms are known as viruses. They are too small to be seen with ordinary microscopes but the most powerful, modern microscopes have brought about some important changes. One of these new instruments is the electron microscope.

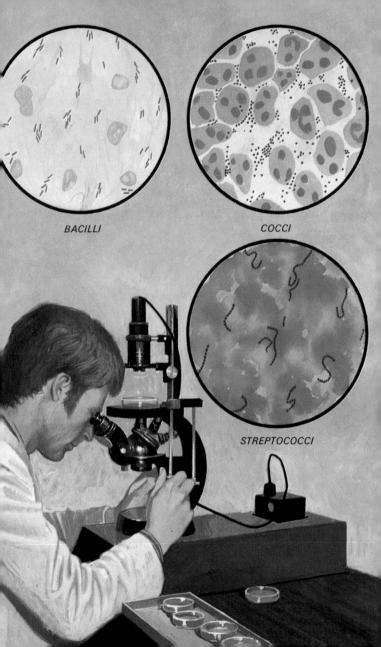

BACILLI

COCCI

STREPTOCOCCI

The electron microscope

The image of an ordinary microscope is made by light waves and these are very short. There are hundreds of thousands to an inch, the different wave-lengths producing the colours of the spectrum. But the microscope which uses light waves cannot show objects below a certain size however much we try to increase the magnification. There is a limit to what light waves can show.

Instead of light rays, the electron microscope uses streams of tiny electrical particles called electrons, and has powerful magnets to direct and focus these just as a lens focusses the light rays in the optical microscope. It can show objects far beyond reach of the lens and magnify one hundred thousand times. Specimens for examination must be cut into sections no thicker than 2 or 3 millionths of an inch and placed in a vacuum.

As you may imagine, this is a microscope for a very special purpose in science, such as the study of bacteria, viruses and the tiny crystals which make up metals.

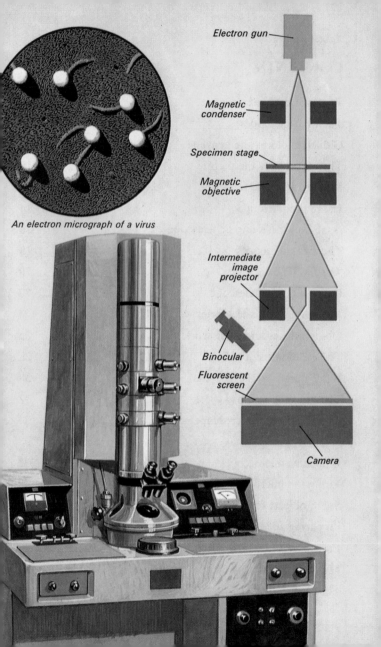

An electron micrograph of a virus

Electron gun

Magnetic condenser

Specimen stage

Magnetic objective

Intermediate image projector

Binocular

Fluorescent screen

Camera

CONTENTS